www.rourkeeducationalmedia.com

Edited by: Keli Sipperley
Cover layout by: Rhea Magaro-Wallace
Interior layout by: Kathy Walsh
Cover and interior illustrations by: Karl West

Library of Congress PCN Data

Elliot Mack, Quarterback / Alisha Gabriel
(Good Sports)
ISBN 978-1-64369-044-5 (hard cover)(alk. paper)
ISBN 978-1-64369-094-0 (soft cover)
ISBN 978-1-64369-191-6 (e-Book)
Library of Congress Control Number: 2018955957

Printed in the United States of America,
North Mankato, Minnesota

Elliot MACK, QUARTERBACK

By Alisha Gabriel
Illustrated by Karl West

Rourke
Educational Media
rourkeeducationalmedia.com

Table of Contents

Chapter One
Don't Worry

I'm Elliot Mack. I just made the Blobfish football team! Coach Goats says most first graders don't play much. But I will. I'm the **quarterback**!

My mom pulls my hair into a ponytail. "Are you ready for your first game?" she asks.

"Yes!" I say. "I can't wait!"

My dad hands me my helmet.
"Are you sure you want to play
football?" he asks.

"Yes!" I say. "Football is fun!"

"I worry you'll get hurt,"

Mom says.

She frowns. "The other team will try to tackle you a lot."

"They have to catch me first!" I say.

Chapter Two
Here Comes Trouble

Uh-oh, here comes trouble,

I think. Mason stops in front

of me. He crosses his arms.

"What are you doing here?"

he asks.

"I made the team," I say.

"Shouldn't you be over there with the cheerleaders?" he asks.

"No. I like playing football," I say.

"Girls don't play football,"
he says.

"I do," I say. "I'm the new
quarterback."

"You're only in first grade.

You're too small," he says.

"They're going to tackle you

over and over."

"Not if you stop them," I say. I smile up at him. "You can cover my blind side," I say. "You're the best **left tackle** on our team."

"Oh, thanks," he says. His
cheeks turn pink.

"That's what makes us a
great team," I say.

"I guess you're right,"
he says.

The cheerleaders wave
their pom-poms. They start
a cheer. "Blobfish rule!
Bulldogs drool!"

Mason shakes his head.

"Who chose blobfish as our

mascot?" he asks. I shrug.

GO BLOBFISH!!

We look up into the stands.
My parents are in the front
row. Mom waves at me. Dad
holds up a camera. "Say
'Blobfish!'" Dad yells.

Mason puts his arm
around me. We smile
and scream, "Blobfish!"

Chapter Three
Secret Weapons

Coach Goats blows his whistle. "**Huddle** up!" he yells. We put on our helmets.

We fist bump our teammates.

Coach Goats says, "Last year the Bulldogs beat us." He rubs his chin. "Why did I tell you that?"

Uh-oh. Some of the players look scared, I think. "That was last year. We're a new team now," I say.

"That's right," Mason says.

He smiles and points at me.

"This year we have a secret

weapon."

I look around. My team is looking at me. "We have a new quarterback," Mason says. "And she's fast."

Coach Goats nods. "You're right. Elliot is a surprise."

I am?

"Each of you can surprise the other team," he says. "Not just Elliot." I smile and nod.

Coach Goats looks at his watch. "Are you ready for our cheer?"

We all put one hand in the middle of the huddle.

"One, two, red and blue,

three, four, watch us score."

"Go Blobfish!"

Bonus Stuff!
Glossary

huddle (HUH-duhl): When a group of people gathers close together.

left tackle (LEFT TAK-uhl): A player that blocks the other team's players. The left tackle protects the quarterback so they have time to throw the ball.

mascot (MAS-kaht): An animal or thing that represents a sports team.

quarterback (KWOR-ter-bak): The quarterback is the player who gets the ball at the start of each play. They pass it, hand it to another player, or run it down the field to score a touchdown.

Discussion Questions

1. How did Elliot feel when she saw Mason walking over? Why do you think she felt this way?

2. What changed when Elliot told Mason he is the best left tackle on the team?

3. How did Mason and Elliot help the team face their fear of the Bulldogs?

Activity:
Folded Paper Football

Fold a piece of paper into a triangle football. Slide it back and forth across a desk to a friend. Take turns making a goal post with your thumbs together and index fingers up. Put one corner of the football on the desk. Then, hold the top corner with a finger. Use the hand you write with to flick the football through the goal post. A flick is like a snap. Touch the nail of your middle finger to the inside of your thumb. Push your finger out fast to flick the football.

Supplies
- one piece of paper
- markers or a pencil
- scissors

Directions
1. Fold a piece of paper in half the long way two times.

2. Fold the top corner to the edge to make a small triangle. Keep folding that triangle down, about seven times.

3. Cut off the extra paper at the bottom. Leave about one inch (2.54 centimeters). Tuck the end paper inside the folded football. Recycle the extra paper.

Writing Prompt

Write a cheer! Use the school colors, the mascot, or names of the characters to create a new cheer. The best cheers are short and rhyme at the end.

About the Author

Alisha Gabriel is a writer, teacher, and reader. As a child, she played many sports, including softball, tennis, and volleyball. She and her husband live near Austin, Texas, where they love tossing the tennis ball to their dogs.

About the Illustrator

Karl West lives and works from a studio on the small island of Portland in Dorset, England. His dogs, Ruby and Angel, lie under his desk while he works, snoring away.